by Oakley Graham

Published by Top That! Publishing plc
Tide Mill Way, Woodbridge, Suffolk, IP12 1AP, UK
www.topthatpublishing.com
Copyright © 2013 Top That! Publishing plc
All rights reserved
0 2 4 6 8 9 7 5 3 1
Printed and bound in China

Creative Director – Simon Couchman
Editorial Director – Daniel Graham

Written by Oakley Graham
Illustrated by Kimberley Scott

ISBN 978-1-78244-220-2

A catalogue record for this book is available from the British Library
Printed and bound in China

*'For my own stubborn little pirates, Noah and Oakie.'*
*Oakley Graham*

On their ships' masts were black flags as dark as the grave,
Striking fear and terror as they sailed through the waves.

This is the tale of two stubborn pirates who just didn't get on,
And their fight is remembered in this pirate shanty song.

Bluebeard owned a map which led to lots of pirate treasure;
More than enough gold and jewels for a life full of pleasure.

Crafty Redbeard stole the map in the dead of the night,
So Bluebeard set sail after him, determined to fight!

'Clear the decks!' fearsome Bluebeard declared;
'Get the boarding-axe sharpened, the cutlasses bared!

Set the cannons ready,
and then quickly bring to me,
The fuse for the cannons,
and the powder-room key!'

Bluebeard's ship was closing in as
Redbeard battled against the tide.
'We'll blow them all to smithereens!
There's nowhere for them to hide!'

For the two stubborn pirates
this really wasn't a game.
Bluebeard ordered his pirates
to get ready and take aim!

'Open the hatches, light the fuses and away with the faint-hearted.'
Bluebeard's fearsome pirate crew prepared to get the battle started!

Pirates loaded the cannons in the gloomy darkness below deck,
While Bluebeard poked and prodded an angry boil on his neck.

And it's down, down,
sink them all down!

Redbeard sensed he was in danger and made a starboard turn,
As cannonballs flew through the air and whistled past the stern.

And it's down, down, sink them all down!

$S$ide by side the ships sailed; both crews calling their war cry,
As the stubborn pirates stood on deck, their cutlasses held high.

'I want my treasure map back!' angry Bluebeard declared.
Redbeard cried, 'Come and get it, unless you're too scared!'

The pirates fought day and night, until both ships were alight.
And when the ships began to sink, they continued with their fight.

And it's down, down, down, sink them all down!

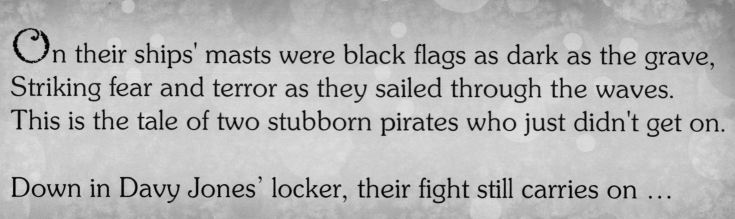

On their ships' masts were black flags as dark as the grave,
Striking fear and terror as they sailed through the waves.
This is the tale of two stubborn pirates who just didn't get on.

Down in Davy Jones' locker, their fight still carries on …